LOVED BEST

LOVED BEST

Patricia C. McKissack

Illustrated by Felicia Marshall

Aladdin

New York   London   Toronto   Sydney

⚱ ALADDIN PAPERBACKS
An imprint of Simon & Schuster Children's Publishing Division
1230 Avenue of the Americas, New York, NY 10020
Text copyright © 2005 by Patricia C. McKissack
Illustrations copyright © 2005 by Felicia Marshall
All rights reserved, including the right of reproduction in whole
or in part in any form.
ALADDIN PAPERBACKS and colophon are registered
trademarks of Simon & Schuster, Inc.
Also available in a paperback edition from Aladdin Paperbacks.
Designed by Tom Daly and Lisa Vega
The text of this book was set in Cheltenham.
Manufactured in the United States of America
First Aladdin Paperbacks edition January 2005
2 4 6 8 10 9 7 5 3 1
The Library of Congress Control Number 2004105885
ISBN 0-689-86152-4 (Library)

In memory of Mrs. Erma Carwell, who loved Pat,
Sarah, and Nolan the best

Chapter 1

At play tryouts Carolyn's friend Janet Parson said her mama loved her best. Since Carolyn was the oldest, she decided her mama must love her the best too. The idea made Carolyn feel strong and important, especially since she'd gotten a speaking part in the upcoming spring play, titled *Mother Nature at Her Best*. The play was about how things in nature worked together for the good of the planet. And how that made Mother Nature happy.

"Mama is going to be so proud of *me*," said Carolyn, skipping out of the community center ahead of her younger brother and sister.

She wasn't going to be a singing bird like her brother, Josh. She wasn't going to be a sunflower like Dana. She had a six-line poem to recite, called "The River."

Janet got a part too. She was going to be the sky.

"Mama will be just as proud of me singing in the bird choir," said Josh.

"There's nothing special about singing *peep, peep, peep* with ten other little kids," said Carolyn, laughing.

"I'm going to be in the sunflower garden and follow the sun," Dana argued. "And that will be fine with Mama."

"Wow, little sister, you've really moved up

in the world. Weren't you a monkey last year?" Carolyn asked, laughing even harder.

Dana poked out her lip and pouted. Josh dropped his head the way he did when he was upset about something. Carolyn didn't notice a thing. "Like I said, Mama is going to be so proud of her favorite child: me!" She enjoyed saying it, because it made her feel strong and important. And Josh reacted exactly the way Carolyn knew he would.

"What makes you think Mama loves you the most?" Josh asked.

Putting her hands on her hips, Carolyn moved in close. Josh stood his ground. "It's real easy to figure out, even for thick heads like you," she said. "I'm nine. You're five. Dana's four. Who has Mama loved the longest?"

Josh refused to answer, so Carolyn did

instead. "Do the math! It was just Mama, Daddy, and me for four whole years before you showed up. So clearly I'm loved more. Duh!"

By that time Granddaddy had turned into the community center driveway. He'd come to pick them up.

"Granddaddy, look," said Carolyn, hopping into the front seat. "I'm going to be the river in the spring play—a speaking part."

Carolyn never noticed that her brother and sister were close to tears.

chapter 2

Granddaddy had agreed to pick up the kids after tryouts and take them to his house. Carolyn loved going to Granddaddy and Grandmama's house. It smelled good all the time, and they played old-fashioned games such as pin the tail on the donkey and hide-and-seek.

The three children were in the backyard playing kickball with Granddaddy. None of them seemed interested in playing ball. They had something else on their minds.

Carolyn spoke up. "If we were all in a boat," she asked Grandaddy, "and the boat was sinking, who would you save first?"

"Me?" shouted Josh. "Me! Me! Me!"

"No, me!" said Dana.

"Everybody knows it would be me," said Carolyn. "I'm the oldest, and that makes me the favorite!"

Granddaddy raised an eyebrow. "Is that right?" he said, wiping his head with the back of his arm. Then he chuckled. "Don't worry about who's going to save you in a sinking boat. Learn how to swim!"

That was such a Granddaddy answer, thought Carolyn. *It made no sense to anybody except him.*

"One day you'll understand," he said, chuckling softly. Maybe so, but not right now.

Carolyn pictured Mama in her mind. Carolyn

and her mother had the same black, curly hair, the same dark eyes, and the same broad smile.

"Don't you think Mama would like the child best who resembles her the most?"

Just then, Grandmama pulled into the driveway. She had bought flowers for her garden.

"Come help me," she called.

The three children looked at each other, and they each knew what the others were thinking.

"Grandmama," Carolyn shouted, racing ahead of her brother and sister. "We've got something to ask you."

Chapter 3

Grandmama said there would be no questions until she took off her shoes and changed into something more comfortable.

In a few minutes she came back outside in her work clothes. She was ready to dig in the dirt and also to listen. "Now, what big question do you have for me?"

"Grandmama," began Carolyn, "which one of us is loved the most?"

"Me," said Josh.

"It's me," said Dana.

"Tell them it's me," said Carolyn.

Grandmama thought for a while. Everybody was quiet, waiting to hear her answer. "Follow me," Grandmama finally said, taking the children to her garden. "I want you to see my spring flowers."

"I'm going to be a sunflower in the play," said Dana. The little girl showed Grandmama how a sunflower's bloom follows the sun across the sky each day.

"I'm going to be in the bird choir," Josh added.

"But I have a speaking part," Carolyn boasted.

Grandmama liked hearing the news. "You all have different parts in the play. That's good." She led them along the winding stone path through the garden. "Variety is good," she added.

Carolyn wondered when Grandmama was

going to answer her question. Instead Grandmama pointed out all the different plants that grew in her garden.

"So many colors. Some big and some small," said Josh.

"They're pretty," said Dana.

"Yes," Grandmama replied. "You three children remind me of these flowers—each one different; each one beautiful; each one loved. No one better than the others."

Carolyn saw Grandmama's large yellow rose bush growing against the garage. She had helped Grandmama plant it when she was four years old. Josh hadn't been born yet. "Grandmama, you told me the yellow rose was special to you and so was I, remember?"

Grandmama had to admit that she was partial to the yellow rose. But Carolyn's interpreta-

tion of what she had said was not what Grandmama had in mind. "These are flowers. You are children," she said quickly. "I love all three of you the same. The same," she added with emphasis.

Just then Daddy came from around the side of the house. He was carrying his suit jacket over his shoulder. "Hey, gang," he called.

"I know who'll have the answer," said Josh.

"Daddy!" they all shouted, and rushed to greet him.

chapter 4

After loading up the car, they started for home, just a few miles away. It was Josh's turn to sit in the front seat. Carolyn and Dana sat in the back.

"I'm going to be a sunflower girl in the play," said Dana. "Are you proud?"

"Of course," answered Daddy.

"Does that mean I'm your favorite?"

"Sure you are," Daddy answered without a moment's thought. Then he threw a kiss to her in the rearview mirror.

Dana threw a kiss back, then gave Carolyn an I-told-you-so look.

"You're very special, honey, because you're my baby girl," Daddy said, smiling.

Josh held his head down again. At a stoplight, Daddy reached over and gave Josh a fake punch on the arm. "Ah, but my only son has got to be the favorite," Daddy said.

A full smile spread across Josh's face, and his almond-shaped eyes sparkled. Carolyn looked like Mama, but Josh was a small version of Daddy. Dana was a combination of both.

Daddy turned down their street. He said to Carolyn over his shoulder, "And you are my favorite big girl, the oldest child, dear to my heart."

"So I am loved best," said Carolyn, filled with excitement.

"That's not what I said." Daddy was confused. He pulled into the driveway and stopped.

Carolyn explained. "What if you and Mama have another baby? Then Dana won't be the baby any more. And what if you and Mama have another baby and it's a boy? Josh won't be the only boy," she said. "But I will *always* be the oldest, so that makes me number one—forever!"

Daddy was dumbfounded. He reported the whole conversation to Mama, who was busy preparing dinner in the kitchen. She stopped stirring a pot and greeted the children. "Carolyn, you've got to stop teasing your brother and sister."

Who was teasing?

Chapter 5

Mama was delighted that all three children had been given parts in the community play.

"I have a speaking part this year," Carolyn said, smiling broadly.

"I'm very, very proud of you," said Mama.

"I'm proud of Josh and Dana, too," she continued, hugging each one of them. Then she scooted them off to wash for dinner.

"Did you hear what Mama said?" Carolyn

asked Josh later when they were watching television. "She said I was her favorite."

Josh turned his back on Carolyn. "Stop saying that. She didn't!" Josh shouted.

Carolyn laughed. "You have to pay attention. Listen. Mama said she was 'very, very proud' of me. But she was just proud of you two. No very, very."

Suddenly Pumpkin the tabby cat leaped into Josh's arms. He purred softly. "I don't want to talk about it anymore," said Josh. "Who cares? Pumpkin is mine. I'm his favorite. Who needs more?"

At bedtime Dana hugged her doll up close. "Does Mama love me just a little bit?" she asked.

Carolyn looked surprised. "I never said she didn't love you guys. Of course she does. I'm just the favorite."

Dana thought about it some more. "I got it," she said. "You're a big girl. It takes a lot more to love you than it does me, 'cause I'm small. But I'll be fine with just a little bit of love."

Chapter 6

Carolyn decided it wasn't necessary to talk about being the favorite anymore. Dana and Josh seemed to accept it, and that was enough for her.

Rehearsals for the spring play were held every Wednesday evening. For the most part, they were going well. Mrs. Lasiter, the play director, was upset that some of the kids hadn't learned their parts. But she praised Carolyn, who had memorized her six-line poem and could recite it from beginning to end without missing a word.

Josh knew the song that the bird choir was going to sing, and Dana practiced hard at being a good sunflower.

Toward the end of one rehearsal, Mrs. Lasiter issued patterns for the costumes. This was always exciting. Dana's costume was a yellow sunflower, with a cut-out in the center for her face. "You should wear a green shirt and green tights," said Mrs. Lasiter.

The little sunflower children were hopping around, squealing and leaping like frogs. Mrs. Lasiter tried to shout over the noise. "I need to see the bird chorus over here," she said, waving her hand over her head.

By that time the bird kids were shouting and jumping like joeys—baby kangaroos. The whole scene was a huge bowl of confusion soup.

When Mrs. Lasiter had given out the costumes, Carolyn realized that she hadn't gotten one. She asked Mrs. Lasiter why.

Mrs. Lasiter nervously thumbed through the pages of her notebook. "You're Carolyn Winters, the river, right?" She checked her notebook once more to be sure. "The river doesn't have a costume," she said.

"What? No costume?" Carolyn was trying not to be rude, but whoever heard of being in a play without a costume? "Mrs. Lasiter," she asked, "why doesn't the river have a costume?"

Mrs. Lasiter was even more anxious, because the little ones were scampering all over the place. "You're one of the older kids with a speaking part, so you don't need a costume."

"But—"

Suddenly there was a bang and a clank. A tulip kid had knocked over a stack of folding chairs and they'd come crashing down. Mrs. Lasiter hurried away, muttering something about "never, ever doing this again."

Dana and Josh were excited to show off their costume patterns to Granddaddy when he picked them up.

"Where's yours, Carolyn?" asked Granddaddy.

It bothered Carolyn that she wasn't going to have a costume. "I don't have to wear one of those goofy-looking getups, because I have a speaking part."

She tried to hide how disappointed she really was.

Chapter 7

During the night, Dana woke up complaining that her stomach ached. Her temperature was high. Mama held Dana in her arms and rocked her back and forth in the rocker—the same one she'd used to rock all three of her children when they were babies. Come morning, Mama took Dana's temperature again and declared that Dana was going to stay home from preschool.

"I'll fix a pot of chicken soup and make tapioca pudding," Mama promised. "That'll make your tummy feel better."

Dana didn't feel good. Her mouth made a smile, but her eyes didn't.

All day, Carolyn thought about how Mama had held Dana in her arms until she fell sleep. She remembered Mama's humming and the melody of the lovely lullaby. That was more than just a little love. It was so obvious. Mama really did adore Dana.

By evening Dana felt much better. She wasn't hot anymore.

Now it was Carolyn's turn. During the night Carolyn forced herself to wake up. She cried out. "Oh, oh, oh! I feel terrible. I'm so, so sick."

Mama took Carolyn's temperature. She felt

her head. "Oh, it's too bad you're not feeling good," said Mama. There was no holding, no rocking, no humming.

Come morning Mama said, "Today is Saturday, and I was going to take all of you to a movie and then for pizza."

Carolyn pulled the covers up to her chin. "Oh, no," she said, sighing deeply. "Now you can't go because you have to stay home and fix me soup and tapioca, right?"

"Wrong," said Mama. "Now *you* have to stay home with the baby-sitter."

Carolyn couldn't believe it. How could Mama leave her when she might have the plague or some other dreaded disease? Instead of seeing a good movie and chowing down on pizza, she was stuck at home . . . on a Saturday. And to make matters worse, she wasn't even sick.

Chapter 8

At play practice on the following Wednesday, Mrs. Lasiter was scurrying about like a mad squirrel, because the little boy bird who was supposed to sing the solo part in the bird choir had an emergency. Now they needed a new lead singer.

"Why don't you let my brother sing the solo?" said Carolyn. "He's pretty good."

Mrs. Lasiter called Josh over to the piano. "Do you think you can do this?" she asked.

"Sure he can," answered Carolyn. Then turning to Josh she added, "Can't you?"

Josh looked too scared to speak.

"My brother is shy sometimes, but he's got a good voice," Carolyn explained, trying to convince Mrs. Lasiter.

Mrs. Lasiter suggested they go through the song one time. Josh was so scared that he was stiff at first. But the more he sang, the more comfortable he became. His voice was clear, and to everyone's surprise, he knew all the words. "I remembered them from practice," he said.

Mrs. Lasiter was relieved that Josh was going to do the solo, and that he was good—even better than the original soloist.

"Told you he could do it," said Carolyn.

Josh was pleased, too, although he would

never admit it. Carolyn could tell because his eyes were round and bright the way they were when he was really happy about something.

"Carolyn, why did you help me? " Josh asked.

Carolyn faked a punch at his shoulder the way Daddy always did. "I'm your big sister. And you should listen to what your big sister says."

"All the time?"

"Most of the time," Carolyn said, laughing. "Make sure you don't goof up and embarrass us all in front of the whole city," she added.

Josh shrugged the way he did when Carolyn got in the last word.

Chapter 9

When Josh told Mama about getting the solo, she baked a chocolate cake, his favorite dessert. *How come he gets a cake for singing a solo?* Carolyn thought. *I didn't get a cake when I got my first speaking part.*

"Josh is blooming," said Mama, her face beaming with pride. Mama pointed to the refrigerator. Josh had gotten all his math problems correct, and his teacher had put a sunshine face on his test paper. Mama had posted his work on the door.

Love was all over her face as she said, "I'm very, very, very proud of him."

Wow! Three verys!

Mama never made a big deal over my perfect papers, Carolyn thought. She was beginning to feel sick to her stomach. Maybe she wasn't numero uno after all.

Not possible, she told herself. *Of course I am.*

A day or two later, Carolyn brought home one of her perfect math papers. "Look, I got one hundred." She showed it to Mama.

"Nice job," she said. "Keep up the good work." That was it?

That was it!

No chocolate cake. No "very, very, very proud of you." Mama didn't put her paper on the refrigerator door either.

Carolyn was beginning to wonder who *was*

loved best? It wasn't her anymore. But maybe she could get back on top if she did well in the play. So she decided to be as good as she could be.

chapter 10

A week before the big play, Mrs. Lasiter scheduled a dress rehearsal. Mama had finished Dana's sunflower costume and Josh's bird costume.

Carolyn decided to be creative with her own. She found a pair of dark blue pants, a light blue shirt, and two blue scarves that she tied at her waist. They fluttered when she walked and reminded her of a flowing river. *Not bad,* she thought, looking in the mirror.

She showed Mrs. Lasiter her design. "What do you think of my idea?"

"Fine, fine, fine," said Mrs. Lasiter, never really taking time to notice. She was off to break up a fight between a mushroom and a tulip.

It was loud and busy as usual, but suddenly Carolyn heard Dana's scream over the other noise. Carolyn rushed to see what was happening. One of the bee boys had snatched Dana's sunflower hat off and ripped it. Dana was wailing at the top of her voice.

"Hey, chill," Carolyn said, pulling Dana off the bee boy, whose wings were bent. "It isn't all that bad."

"It's not?" Dana said tearfully.

Carolyn examined the rip in the sunflower. "Hey, I put together my own costume, so I can fix this one. All I need is a needle and thread."

"Here, I have a sewing kit in my purse," said Mrs. Lasiter. "Thanks for taking care of this, Carolyn. You're a lifesaver."

Dana's eyes were wide with concern. "Will it be a'right?"

"Yeah! I got you covered. Now, stop being such a crybaby!"

Dana smiled.

Chapter 11

On the evening of the program, everybody began arriving at the community center. The room was fully decorated like a bright spring day. Bees were buzzing, birds were chirping, and rabbits were hopping about. Then it was showtime. "Break a leg, everybody," whispered Mrs. Lasiter nervously.

The audience sang the "Star-Spangled Banner" way off-key. Somebody else gave a welcome. And the play began.

The first scene up was performed by Dana's age group. The sunflower garden.

Dana and all ten of the little three- through five-year-old sunflowers followed the six-year-old sun across the sky. White fluffy clouds hung from the ceiling, and a carpet of green grass covered the floor.

Carolyn looked from behind the big sheet that served as a curtain. Mama was smiling as she watched little Dana lean toward the sun just as a real flower does.

Daddy was busy taking video, never missing a minute of it. Granddaddy was enjoying himself too. He was snapping pictures, one after the other. *She is cute,* thought Carolyn. *But wait until it's my turn. I'm going to blow them all away.*

When it was Josh's turn Carolyn could see Mama holding her breath, especially when it was time for Josh to sing. He was so good. Not one mistake. Daddy got so involved with listening, he almost forgot to start the camera. In fact Grandmama took over the video so Daddy could concentrate on Josh's performance.

At the end Josh stepped forward and took a bow. Everybody cheered and applauded. Carolyn applauded and yelled out a big, "Yo, bro!" Josh heard her and grinned. He'd never looked happier.

Wait till I do my thing, though, thought Carolyn.

There was a brief intermission while the set was changed. Then it was time for the older children. Carolyn lined up behind Greg Stewart, who was the mountain. Debra Miller, who was the valley, and Janet Parson, who was the sky, were behind Carolyn.

Greg finished his poem. Then Carolyn heard

her name announced. She stepped onstage like she had at practice many times. But this time, she didn't see the microphone cord, and she tripped. People laughed, and that made her nervous.

She looked at the audience. There were so many people in the room. And they were all looking at her. It wasn't like practice, when kids were running around making noise and nobody was paying attention. Now every eye was on her, including Mama's, Daddy's, Granddaddy's, and Grandmama's.

Carolyn searched for the first words of the poem, but she couldn't remember them.

"I am the river," Mrs. Lasiter whispered from offstage. Everybody heard her, and they laughed again.

"I ... am ... the river," said Carolyn. The microphone squeaked and she jumped. More laughter.

Where were the words? Her memory was like a blank sheet of paper. Nothing.

How many times had she said that dumb poem? She wanted the earth to open up and swallow her whole. "I can't remember. . . ." She sobbed.

Then someone began to applaud. She had seen that done for little kids who messed up. This wasn't supposed to happen—not to her.

Feeling humiliated and not knowing what to do, she ran. Bounding offstage, she bolted for the side door and rushed into the parking lot.

Strong arms caught her just as she collapsed beside the family car. "Carolyn." It was Mama who held her tightly. Mama's voice was as soothing as a warm breeze. "You're going to be fine, daughter. Just fine."

Chapter 12

At that moment Carolyn's world seemed over. How do you go on when you've made such a mess of things? She couldn't stop crying. "I know I'm not loved most. But can you still love me at all after messing up?"

Mama sighed. "Where do you get such ideas? You are my daughter, and I love you very much."

Carolyn sniffed. "Just one very."

Mama didn't get it. "Carolyn, why are you so concerned about being loved the most and being the favorite?

"Well, Janet Parson said she was her mama's favorite."

"For goodness' sake, Carolyn! Janet is an only child."

Carolyn shrugged. "Well, I was the only child for four years. So I decided I was your favorite because you'd loved me longest. But then . . ." Carolyn's voice trailed off.

"Then what?" Mama was ready to listen. She leaned against the car with her arms folded.

Carolyn told her everything.

"You treated Dana special when she was sick. But when I was sick, you didn't make soup and pudding and sing to me."

"You weren't really sick," Mama said, chuckling. "Remember the boy who cried wolf when no wolf was coming?"

Carolyn knew that story from school. "Nobody believed him when the wolf really came."

Mama smiled. "And you shouldn't pretend to be sick unless you really are. When you are sick, I'll do the soup thing."

"Okay." Carolyn agreed she was wrong. "But," she continued, "you put Josh's paper on the refrigerator and fixed him a cake for getting the singing part. But you didn't put my paper up there."

Mama didn't hesitate. "You've had your fair share of papers on the refrigerator. Josh is so shy. Things don't come easy for him like they do for you. So when I saw him trying new things and getting a perfect paper, I thought he needed extra attention."

Mama handed Carolyn tissues. Carolyn blew her nose on one and dried her eyes with the other. "I'm sorry," she said.

Mama looked Carolyn in the eye. "I could never love one of my children *more* than the other. But all three of you are loved the *best* I know how."

Suddenly a sunflower and a bird appeared around the side of the car.

"Don't cry, Carolyn," said Dana. "It will be okay."

"Come on, Carolyn. Don't give up. You wouldn't let me give up," said Josh. "You're our big sister, the only one we have."

Just then Dad found them. And behind him were Grandmama and Granddaddy.

"Carolyn," Daddy said, "do you think, maybe, you might want to try doing your poem again?

Mrs. Lasiter said you could go on after the sky."

Carolyn thought about it. Mama gave her an encouraging nod. "You know who's loved best?" Carolyn said.

"No. Who?" the family asked.

"You are all loved best," said Carolyn, winking at Mama. Then she went back inside with her scarves flowing like a river.

Don't miss another wonderful story by Patricia C. McKissack!

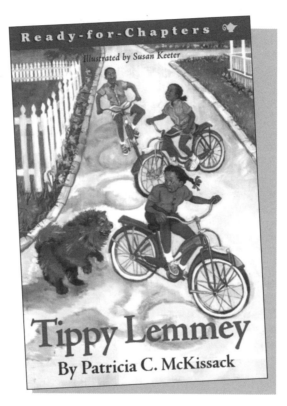

Tippy Lemmey, the story of a very special dog

Aladdin Paperbacks · Simon & Schuster Children's Publishing
www.SimonSaysKids.com

A r e Y o u
Ready-for-Chapters 🫖

Page-turning step-up books for kids ready to tackle something more challenging than beginning readers

The Cobble Street Cousins
by Cynthia Rylant
illustrated by
Wendy Anderson Halperin
#1 In Aunt Lucy's Kitchen
0-689-81708-8
#2 A Little Shopping
0-689-81709-6
#3 Special Gifts
0-689-81715-0

The Werewolf Club
by Daniel Pinkwater
illustrated by Jill Pinkwater
#1 The Magic Pretzel
0-689-83790-9
#2 The Lunchroom of Doom
0-689-83845-X

Third-Grade Detectives
by George Edward Stanley
illustrated by
Salvatore Murdocca
#1 The Clue of the Left-Handed Envelope
0-689-82194-8
#2 The Puzzle of the Pretty Pink Handkerchief
0-689-82232-4

Annabel the Actress:
Starring in Gorilla My Dreams
by Ellen Conford
illustrated by
Renee W. Andriani
0-689-83883-2

The Courage of Sarah Noble
by Alice Dalgliesh
0-689-71540-4

The Bears on Hemlock Mountain
by Alice Dalgliesh
0 689-71604-4

Ready-for-Chapters

ALADDIN PAPERBACKS
Simon & Schuster Children's Publishing • www.SimonSaysKids.com